the Sandbox

A Story of Inclusion and Embracing Differences

Written by **Carolyn and Amelia Furlow**

Illustrated by **Madison Revis**

Distributed by Bublish, Inc.

978-1-64704-160-1 (Paperback)
978-1-64704-161-8 (Hardback)
978-1-64704-162-5 (eBook)

This collection is dedicated to my bouncing
granddaughter, Imani Smiles.
A beautiful brown baby with curious eyes.
She seeks truth and joy when in your lap she arrives.
Giggles, kisses, and hugs she provides.
I pray life gives her a joyful ride.

We also dedicate this series to my oldest daughter,
Barbara Furlow-Smiles, Imani's mom. She is the
glue that brings it all together. Like a diamond
sparkling from every side her spirit shines and
offers light to everyone she encounters.

Foreword

The Sandbox is an enlightened, uniquely, creative story which represents the world in its authentic form of diversity. The children in this book are all from different races and cultures. Children are taught through this story to celebrate and embrace differences. *The Sandbox* joins in on the Renaissance to counter and dispel negative imagery and literature of people of color.

Concepts at the beginning of a life can carry through a person's lifetime. This is why it is critical to address simple messages of kindness and respect on the onset of children's development. Through this book children and parents can open their minds to see the unique characteristics of one another as opposed to a stereo type.

Michael Eric Dyson, Ph.D.
Professor of Sociology at Georgetown, University
Author of *Tears We Cannot Stop: Sermon to White America*

One day, Imani looked up at the big, yellow sun.
She felt warm rays kiss her cheeks.
What a beautiful day, she thought.

I think I will take a walk, she said to herself.
All of my friends will be at the park,
And we love playing in the sandbox.

Look, there goes Alba!
Imani ran toward her friend.
"Are you going to the park, Alba?"
"Yes," Alba answered and smiled.
"Great! We can walk together," Imani said.

3

The two girls started walking.
One step, two steps, three steps.
"Look up at the big, green tree!" Imani shouted.
"It's so pretty!" Alba exclaimed as they skipped along.

Imani studied Alba and said, "Alba, your hair is straight."
Alba nodded. "Yes, and your hair is curly, Imani."
"And look, our skin is different, too," Imani added. "I'm brown and you're beige!"
"That's awesome!"

Suddenly, their friend, Tao jumped out from
behind the tree. "Boo!"
Imani screamed and Alba started to run away.
Tao laughed. "Don't be scared! It's only me."

"Are you on the way to the park?" Imani asked Tao.

"Yes, I am."

"Good!" said Alba. "We can all walk together. Look, Imani. Tao has black hair, too. But his eyes are different from yours and mine."

"But they're still pretty, like flowers in a garden," Imani said.

"What does that mean? I'm not a flower," Tao pouted.

"Of course not," Alba and Imani said together.

"But we're like all the flowers in the garden," said Imani. "Isn't it beautiful?"

"Hey!" Ella came running down the sidewalk. "Wait up, guys! I want to walk with you."

"Hi Ella!" The three friends were happy to see her.

"Come play with us in the sandbox," Tao said.

"Look, Alba," Imani said. "Ella's hair is yellow and straight."

"And her eyes are blue," added Alba.

"We all look different," Tao laughed, "but that's what makes it fun."

"Yes," Alba smiled. "She's another flower in our garden."

Imani's eyes twinkled. "Our garden is full of many colors and different types of flowers."

Happily, they exclaimed, "That's awesome!"

"I like flowers," said Ella. "What flower am I?"

"You're a daffodil," they all said together.

Tao did flips and the three girls skipped along holding hands.

"Look, there's the park!" Imani pointed.

Wiz was sitting on the edge of the sandbox.
"Hi guys. Look at the bugs I caught."
One, two, three. Wiz pointed at the bugs in his bottle.
They each looked different.

The first was a pretty butterfly with many colors.
The second was a brown, black and tan beetle.
The third was a bright green grasshopper.
They were all different and they were each beautiful.

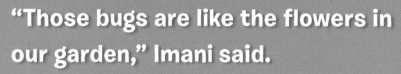

"Those bugs are like the flowers in
our garden," Imani said.
"They are all different."
"And they're all beautiful!" exclaimed Alba.
The five friends laughed and played in the sandbox.

"Look," Ella said, "Wiz's hair is bright red."
"It's curly, too," Imani added. "And his eyes are blue."
"What kind of flower is Wiz?" Alba smiled.
"I think he's a rose."

The children laughed and told Wiz about how they were all like flowers in a garden.

Abul's long black hair blew back as he ran and jumped into the sandbox. "Hey everybody. What are you doing?"

"We are playing in the sandbox," Wiz responded.

"You can play with us."

Everyone welcomed Abul with smiles.

"Look, Abul is different, too. He is a boy with long black hair," Alba explained.

Tao questioned, "Can you imagine what it would be like if we all looked the same?"

"B-O-R-I-N-G!" They all shouted.

"I am happy we all look different," Ella said.
Imani clapped her hands. "We're like all the different colored flowers in the garden."

Everyone shouted,
"That's awesome!
Let's go play in the sandbox together!"

Author Bios

Carolyn Furlow received a Master of Arts degree in Creative Writing. She is the mother of 3 adult children and a grandmother to one darling granddaughter, Imani. As a teacher she has experienced first-hand the faces of isolation on students who feel disconnected to the lessons and reading materials in their classrooms. In a spirit of love and high regard for all children, she and her daughter, Amelia Furlow, have created a series of stories which speaks to all children and allows them to feel connected to the stories they read in classrooms and at home. The world is a visible melting pot of beautiful children across the globe. Our stories reflect their presence and fosters acceptance and respect for differences.

Amelia Furlow is a Marriage and Family therapist intern. Recognizing a need for more diverse stories to be told within Children's Books, she collaborated with her mother, Carolyn Furlow, to create a series that highlight the similarities as well as the individuality of human beings. Telling stories that celebrate one's uniqueness engages young minds to read. Amelia experienced the power of diversity at a very young age. Today, more than ever, children need to feel included. This series surely will bring cheer to those who read it!